Summer Love

Based on the TV series *Hey Arnold!*®
created by Craig Bartlett as seen on *Nickelodeon*®

SIMON SPOTLIGHT
An imprint of Simon & Schuster Children's Publishing Division
1230 Avenue of the Americas, New York, New York 10020

Manufactured in the United States of America

First Edition
2 4 6 8 10 9 7 5 3 1

ISBN 0-689-83937-5

Library of Congress Control Number 00-111803

HEY ARNOLD! ™

Summer Love

by **Craig Bartlett** and **Maggie Groening**

based on a screenplay by
Michelle Lamoreaux and **Joseph Purdy**

interiors illustrated by **Tim Parsons**
cover illustrated by **Tuck Tucker,**
Kenji Notani, and **Teale Wang**

Simon Spotlight/Nickelodeon

New York   London   Toronto   Sydney   Singapore

CHAPTER 1

"Finally!" Arnold smiled as he walked out the front door of P.S. 118. "Vacation at last!"

"I love it," Gerald agreed. "A whole entire summer away from homework, teachers, and—"

"Watch your back! Watch your back! Outta my way!" Helga plowed through the door behind them and crashed right into Arnold. They tumbled down the steps and lay sprawled at the bottom in a tangle of arms and legs.

"Nice going, football head!"

"Hey, you're the one who knocked me down, Helga!"

"Yeah, well, that's because I'm trapped in school every day with a bunch of losers, and when vacation finally comes, I want to get outta here as fast as I can. Got it, loser?"

"Helga, what're you so mad about?" Arnold said.

"I'll tell you what I'm *glad* about, monkey face: This first week of summer vacation is going to be the best ever, because I'll be far, far away from you." Scowling furiously, she stomped off.

But as soon as she got around the corner, Helga ducked into a secluded doorway and pulled out her hidden locket. She gazed lovingly at the class picture of Arnold glued inside.

"Oh, Arnold!" she whispered. "How cruel

I am each and every time I see you. How brutally I lash out, stupidly widening our already gigantic rift."

She sighed ruefully. "And now, my love . . . now I must spend an entire week of our summer apart from you—doomed to obsessively relive my most regrettable behavior the whole time!"

Helga peeked furtively around the corner. Arnold and Gerald were coming. She shrank farther back into the doorway so they wouldn't notice.

"Man, Arnold," Gerald said as they passed. "That Helga G. Pataki is one person I will not miss—ever."

"I agree, Gerald. I definitely agree," Arnold said.

The next morning Grandpa's Packard was filled to bursting as it roared out of town.

Grandma and Arnold were crammed in the front seat with Grandpa, and all the boarders were squished together in the back.

"Boy, Grandpa, this is gonna be great," Arnold said. "I can't wait to get to the beach."

"Ah, my beloved beach," Grandpa sighed happily. "I had such fun there as a young boy, romping around the dunes, eating snails and seaweed, making a skirt out of shells and dancing for the visiting sailors. The beach has such a magical, romantic quality."

"Romantic, huh?" Susie Kokoshka said hopefully. She nudged Oskar.

"Ehh . . ." Oskar shrugged. "I just want to find a treasure chest buried in the sand."

"Buried treasure? Ha!" Ernie snorted. "What an imbecile. Everyone knows the beach is a place for passion."

He reached over the front seat to slap Arnold on the shoulder. "Hey Arnold, maybe this beach vacation will be good to you, romantically speaking, you know?"

"I'm just planning to hang out and have fun, Mr. Potts," Arnold said uncomfortably. "I'm not really looking to make any new friends."

"I don't blame you, short man," Grandpa said. "Heck, I don't even want to see the people I already know." He glanced in the rearview mirror at the backseat. "Got that?"

At that same moment, on the same highway, Helga was sprawled in the backseat of her parents' Lincoln, watching her portable TV and trying to ignore the conversation in the front.

"This is gonna be great, Miriam!" Big Bob yelled. "A whole entire week of hanging out at the beach!"

"But I just really hate the beach so much," Miriam protested weakly. "The sun and the sand

and the water and all those loud, happy people—"

"Well, get over it, Miriam, 'cause that's where we're going."

Suddenly the theme music for Helga's favorite show, *Babewatch,* started, and Helga stared intently at her little TV. Watching the swimsuit-clad actors running on the sand, she slipped into her favorite daydream: Helga and Arnold, bodacious and buff, running along the sand and smiling dreamily at one another.

CHAPTER 2

The rental beach house was a gray shingled duplex, a little weathered, but cozy. Within minutes of their arrival, the boarding house gang were ready for vacation to start.

Grandpa unpacked his fishing gear. Grandma waxed her surfboard. Susie pulled out the first of her stack of romance novels and found a comfy chair on the porch. Arnold, Ernie, Mr. Hyunh, and Oskar emerged from the house dressed in shorts and sunglasses.

"Well, we're off to mingle," Ernie announced.

"Yes! To meet big, beautiful ladies!" agreed Mr. Hyunh as he and Ernie trotted down the path toward town.

Susie called from the porch. "So you're going to town too, Oskar, and leaving me here all alone?"

"Okay, sounds good to me," Oskar said, and he sprinted to catch up with Ernie and Mr. Hyunh.

Arnold looked around and noticed a pail and shovel in a corner of the porch. He picked them up. "Okay . . . I guess I'll make sand castles." He walked down to the beach, breathed the fresh sea air, and smiled contentedly.

Arnold scanned the beach looking for the right spot to start his castle, then shrugged and dropped the bucket where he was standing. As he began digging, a car pulled up to the other side of the duplex.

The driver's side door opened. "We're here!" Big Bob Pataki bellowed.

Miriam woke up and looked out the window blearily. "Huh? Where am I?"

Helga squinted at the beach house from her window. "Oh, man. What a dump." She climbed out of the car, glanced at the ocean and sighed. "This is gonna be the worst week of my entire life. Bob, Miriam, and a skanky old shack hours away from Arnold."

"Helga?" Arnold said. "What are you doing here?"

CHAPTER 3

Helga spun around. Arnold was right behind her! "Arnold?!" she squeaked, then quickly snapped back to her usual Helga self. "I mean . . . whaddaya mean, what am I doing here? What are *you* doing here, football head?"

"My grandpa brought us here for the week." Arnold stared at Helga in amazement. "Wow, talk about a coincidence. I mean, what are the odds that we'd wind up at the same exact beach house?"

Helga snorted. "Yeah, well . . . don't get any ideas about being all chummy with me, hair boy. I mean, just because we're staying in the same duplex doesn't mean we're suddenly friends or anything. As a matter of fact, I still hate your stinking guts, so you better just stay the heck out of my way. Got it?" She wheeled around and stomped into the house.

"Fine with me, Helga," Arnold said as he turned back to his sand castle.

Once inside the beach house, Helga dashed up to her room and peeked out at Arnold from the curtained window. "What is the matter with me?" she wailed. "Why do I always have to be such a jerk to Arnold? I mean, here I am alone at the beach with the guy and what do I do? I barrage him with insults and push him away!"

She put her face in her hands. "Man, talk

about an idiot—this is my big chance and I'm totally blowing it!" She yanked the curtain open. Down on the beach, Arnold was peacefully working on his sand castle.

"That's it," muttered Helga fiercely. "I'm through being a psychotic freak. From now on, I'm going to be . . . nice." The last word came out in a hiss. "This is gonna be the best vacation of my life, and nothing or nobody is gonna stand in my way."

The surf rumbled in the distance as Arnold dug contentedly in the sand. Suddenly a shadow fell over him. "That is a fantastic sand castle," someone said.

Arnold turned to see a girl, maybe eleven or twelve years old. Her long, blond hair was backlit by the sun. She wore shorts and a tank top, and smiled sweetly down at him.

Arnold just stared back. The girl was so

perfect and so lovely. "Thanks," he finally mumbled.

"My name's Summer. What's yours?"

"Arnold."

"Well, Arnold, you must be a great artist, because that's the best sand castle I've ever seen."

"Really?" Arnold said, looking at it doubtfully.

"Yes, really. In fact, I bet you'd be a shoo-in at the sand castle competition at the Beach Festival this weekend."

"A sand castle competition? I didn't know there was one."

At that moment Helga came out of the beach house, still muttering to herself. "Now, remember, Helga, just stick to the plan. . . ." She looked up and her eyes bugged out; there was Arnold, talking to an annoyingly beautiful girl! Helga jumped back into the shadow of the porch to watch.

"Well, you really should think about it, Arnold," Summer was saying. "Because you do awesome things with sand." She reached over and gently touched his hair. "And in the meantime, you can show me around the beach, since I'm new around here."

"Actually," Arnold said, "I've never been here before either. I'm just here for the week."

"Perfect!" Summer smiled her perfect smile at him. "We can explore together then."

"'You do awesome things with sand?'" Helga hissed. "Criminey! What the heck is going on here? I'm gone for two lousy minutes, and all of a sudden this bimbo is moving in on my territory!"

She glowered, hands on her hips. "Well, Arnold is going to be mine this vacation. Just let her try and *explore* with him. I'll make her so miserable, she'll wish she never set foot on this beach!"

CHAPTER 4

Oskar, Ernie, and Mr. Hyunh strode along the boardwalk, ready for action. A sign outside a T-shirt shop instantly caught Oskar's eye. "Want to find coins, jewelry, and other valuables on the beach?" Oskar slowly read aloud. "Rent a metal detector for only $9.99!"

As if on cue, the alert shop owner came out, holding a metal detector out to Oskar. "That's right, sir, only $9.99. And you get to keep everything it finds."

Oskar seized the metal detector. "I get to keep everything it finds? It's a deal!" He pointed to Ernie. "That man over there will give you the money." Oskar scurried off in the direction of the beach before Ernie realized what had happened.

The detector was successful beyond Oskar's wildest dreams. Within minutes, he discovered astonishing amounts of treasure tucked in the belongings of rows of napping sunbathers. As he walked along, the detector ticked as it uncovered watches, bracelets, rings, and loose change.

"This metal detector works great!" Oskar chuckled as he stuffed his pockets. "It finds so many hidden valuables!"

Meanwhile, not far away, Mr. Hyunh and Ernie had dug a deep hole in the sand. When it was four feet deep, Ernie jumped into it.

"Will this work?" Mr. Hyunh asked.

"Positive, Hyunski. When women see a guy buried up to his head in the sand, they come over, and that's when you start chatting 'em up and turning on the charm! I know—that's how my father met my mother. Now, bury me."

Mr. Hyunh began pushing sand back into the hole, burying Ernie up to his neck. Then he stood back and admired the effect.

"Oooh, this is a great photo opportunity! I want to get my camera. I will be right back!"

"All right, but make it snappy," Ernie called after him, then turning to a passerby, yelled out, "Good afternoon, miss! You're looking lovely."

The girl looked down at Ernie's head in the sand and stepped back in shock. "Eeeew," she said, and quickly walked away.

Ernie tried the same line a few more times with other ladies as they passed, but didn't have better luck. Eventually he grew bored and discouraged. "Where the heck is Hyunh? How long does it take to find a camera?"

Ernie struggled to get out of the sand, but couldn't budge. He craned his neck as much as he could and called a little louder. "Hey, uh, anyone? I'm buried up to my neck here! A little help?"

Suddenly three tough-looking kids loomed over him. "Hey, ugly dude," said one. "We'll help." He picked up a nearby pail and set it over Ernie's head.

"Wait . . . no!" Ernie's voice was muffled by the pail. The kids laughed and wandered off down the beach.

When Mr. Hyunh finally returned with his camera, Ernie was nowhere to be seen. He looked all around, scratching his head.

"I thought I left him right here," he said,

then continued down the beach, anxiously searching. He didn't hear the voice that had called faintly nearby: "Hyunh, is that you? I'm under the bucket! Help!"

CHAPTER 5

Later that afternoon Arnold and Summer went floating on a rubber raft. "Mmm . . . there's just something so relaxing about the ocean, don't you think, Arnold?" Summer said dreamily.

Behind them a few yards away, Helga slowly surfaced wearing a mask and snorkel. "Oh, I wouldn't get too relaxed if I were you, honey," she said softly. Helga took a deep breath, then ducked under the water to fire a dart at the raft with a blowgun.

There was a loud *pop!* and the raft began to deflate quickly. Arnold and Summer splashed frantically and scrambled to shore, their peaceful idyll destroyed.

Helga chuckled to herself. "Perfect," she said.

But Summer and Arnold didn't let that spoil their day together; they dried off and headed to lunch at a beachside restaurant and ordered the lobster special.

Helga wasn't going to have her day spoiled either. She ducked into the restaurant kitchen and looked around. Live lobsters wriggled in tanks while others boiled in pots. "Lobster special, huh?" Helga grinned slyly. "I've got a real special lobster for ya, toots."

As a waiter plopped a cooked lobster onto a tray and covered it, Helga reached into the tank and came up with a snapping live one.

She slipped it under the lid of the serving dish as the waiter walked outside to Arnold and Summer's table. Helga snuck out the door after him, hiding behind a large bush.

When the waiter lifted the lid, the lobster immediately grabbed tightly onto Summer's hair with both claws. The sound of Summer's terrified scream was music to Helga's ears.

But even this couldn't ruin Arnold and Summer's day. That afternoon they were still together, lying side by side on beach blankets in the sun.

"Isn't this amazing, Arnold?" Summer said, smiling. "Just you and me . . . hanging out together."

"Yeah." Arnold glanced shyly at Summer. "And . . . even though some crazy things happened . . . I'm still really glad I met you, Summer."

"Oh, me too, Arnold, me too."

"You're just so much nicer than the girls at my school." Arnold took a deep breath, and then he said it: "And well, the truth is . . . I really like you a lot."

Summer smiled back. "And I really like you, Arnold. I feel like we have something special." Summer took Arnold's hand and held it. "This may sound silly, but I've never felt so comfortable with a boy before."

"I wouldn't get too comfortable, sweetheart," muttered Helga as she crouched behind a nearby lifeguard stand, watching them intently.

Arnold and Summer both lay facedown on their beach blankets, dozing in the sun. Helga tiptoed over to them and scattered pieces of bread from a sack, all around the edges of the blanket. Then she dashed back behind the lifeguard stand and waited.

Within moments, dozens of hungry seagulls began to swarm and screech over the scattered bread. Arnold and Summer jumped up in horror as the birds swooped and squawked at them. "Eeeeek! Help! Get 'em off me!" Summer shrieked as they ran for cover by the lifeguard kayaks.

They gasped for breath for a moment. "Are you okay?" Arnold said. Then he heard hysterical laughter coming from somewhere behind the lifeguard station.

Helga was rolling on the sand, cackling to herself. "Ha! This is the best one yet! I mean, sure, the lobster and the raft were pretty funny, but this takes the cake!"

Arnold tapped her on the shoulder. "Helga? I heard everything you just said."

Helga stopped laughing abruptly. "Uh . . . I . . . you did?"

"Yeah. So if you're through being mean to me and Summer for no reason at all, I'd really appreciate it if you'd take your own advice and just stay out of my way. For good." He walked away, leaving Helga dazed and crushed.

Summer walked up to Arnold. "Who was that?" she asked.

"Just one of those girls from my school I was telling you about," Arnold said.

CHAPTER 6

The wind was starting to pick up. Sand blew down the beach, and suddenly the pail blew off Ernie's head.

"Whoo—free at last!" he exclaimed. "It was getting pretty clammy in there!" Ernie squinted in the brightness. Just then someone plopped a beach chair directly over his head. An extremely large sunbather settled into the chair and Ernie disappeared under it. "Mmmmmphhhh!" groaned Ernie.

Mr. Hyunh walked by again. "Hello? Mr. Potts?" he called anxiously. "Where are you, Ernie?"

In despair Helga slumped at the end of a pier and watched the sun set slowly into the ocean. "Why am I such an idiot? Why have I allowed my casual cruelties to push Arnold away from me?"

She pulled out her locket and gazed at Arnold's picture. "Oh, my darling! If only you knew how sorry I am. If only you knew how deeply I regret any pain I may have unintentionally inflicted on you and your innocent yet trampy little friend, Summer—"

Just then Helga heard laughter directly beneath her. She peeked through the planks: there was Summer, with a boy her age.

"It's all working out just like we planned, Sandy," she was saying. "Arnold thinks I

really, really like him. I have him convinced that he's, like, the most special boy I've ever met!"

"Whoa," Sandy said. "He's, like, stupider than I ever could've imagined."

"Tell me about it," Summer said, laughing. "The kid's an idiot. Anyway, I'll flirt with him one more day and then get him to agree to build me a killer sand castle at the Beach Festival. With his help, I'll easily win first place."

Sandy pulled a Beach Festival flyer out of his back pocket. He pointed to it and added, "Then you'll dump Arnold the sucker and win the grand prize—a guest appearance on *Babewatch*."

Summer smiled and flipped back her hair.

"And your acting career will skyrocket! And I'll be your manager."

"Right." Summer put her arms around Sandy's neck and kissed him. Sandy carelessly dropped the flyer as they walked back toward the dunes, holding hands.

Stunned, Helga watched them walk away. Then she looked down at her locket. "Oh, my dear, cherished, naive Arnold, I can't stand idly by and let you be eaten alive by Summer's sadistic plot. I must take action!"

She picked up the Beach Festival flyer and studied it. "Besides, getting a part on *Babewatch* is my fantasy! No way she's horning in on that, too!"

CHAPTER 7

Oskar was very pleased with his metal detector; his pockets were sagging with all the treasure it had picked up. As he shuffled along with the machine, he passed a flyer stapled to a telephone pole. It was from the police department: "Caution! Beware of beach thief."

"Oh, this is terrible!" Oskar exclaimed. "A thief on the beach? Oh, I hope someone catches this awful, criminal person."

Just then the metal detector began ticking rapidly and Oskar looked down. It was pulling the change from the pocket of a man sleeping in a deck chair. "Oh, goody!" Oskar whispered. "More treasure!"

"Hold it right there, sir," a policeman said, walking up behind Oskar. The policeman was followed by a group of angry tourists. "Would you mind emptying your pockets?"

"That's my watch he's wearing, right there!" a man yelled angrily, pointing at Oskar's wrist.

"What, my treasure?" Oskar said, looking at the watch. "My metal detector found it on the beach. Is it yours?" He handed the watch to the man.

The policeman began to snap handcuffs on Oskar when the metal detector began to tick loudly again. Oskar, the policeman, and the tourists all turned to look. The detector

was pointing toward a large sunbather in a beach chair. "Look, it's finding something else!" Oskar exclaimed.

A faint, muffled cry came from beneath the beach chair. "Sir, would you kindly step aside?" the policeman asked the sunbather. When the chair was moved, there was Ernie's head!

"Ohhh! Ahhhhh!" Ernie gasped, blinking and shaking his head. "What took you so long?"

He was quickly pulled out of the sand. As he brushed himself off, Mr. Hyunh came running back. "Oh, Ernie, you are safe! I was so worried about you! Are you okay?"

"I'm fine," Ernie said. "A little woozy and my bladder's pretty full, but I'm fine." He knocked on the side of his head. "Good thing I've got this steel plate in my head or Kokoshka would never have found me, huh?"

43

"Oh, yes! Aren't you going to thank me, my dear, tiny friend Ernie?" Oskar interjected quickly. He shook the handcuffs on his hands. "I was looking all over for you with my metal detector."

The policeman looked at Oskar in surprise. "Is that what you were doing this whole time?"

"Absolutely!"

"Well, in that case, you're a hero!" the policeman said. The crowd, which had been angry at Oskar the moment before, started to cheer.

After a while the crowd dispersed and Susie arrived. "Oskar? What's going on?" she asked.

"Oh, Susie!" Oskar said. "I found you a present with my metal detector!" He handed her a jeweled brooch.

Susie smiled and her eyes filled with tears as she took the present. "Oh, Oskar!" She sniffed happily. Then she looked at it more closely. "'To Patricia from Edward'?"

CHAPTER 8

It was night when Helga got back to the duplex—Arnold's window was dark.

Helga gathered a handful of pebbles from the driveway and began flinging them up at Arnold's window. "Open up, Arnold, it's important!" she called.

Finally a light came on and Arnold appeared at the window. He was annoyed. "What do you want, Helga?"

"I want to apologize, Arnold. I mean, you

were right—I was being mean to you and Summer for no reason at all. But the good news is, it's okay!"

"It is?"

"Yes, it's perfectly fine because, the thing is, I just heard Summer talking, and it turns out she's actually evil! And she's got this whole crazy plot against you!"

Arnold gave her a half-lidded look and let out a bored sigh. "Helga, give it up."

"But you don't understand," Helga cried. "I'm telling you the truth! Summer is a monster, Arnold. A horrible, scheming monster!"

"Sure, Helga." Arnold rolled his eyes. "I gotta go." He slammed the window shut and turned away. The light in the room went off.

"Criminey! I've got to make him listen to me!" Helga wailed.

The next morning Arnold and Summer sat together at the end of the pier, their feet dangling over the water.

"Oh, Arnold. We're having such an incredible week, aren't we?" Summer cooed.

"Yeah."

Summer suddenly sat up straight. "Hey! I know the perfect way to capture it! Come on!" She jumped up and dashed down the pier.

As Arnold rose to follow, he heard whispering. Arnold looked down to see Helga peering up at him through the slats of the pier. "I'm telling you, Arnold. Don't listen to her! She's a liar! She's just using you. . . ."

Disgusted, Arnold shook his head and started walking away.

"Don't go, Arnold!" Helga called out. "I swear, she's up to no good! She's a man-eater!" A sudden wave washed in and drenched her, and when Helga could see through her sodden hair again, Summer had taken Arnold's arm and they were walking toward the beach.

"Come on, Arnold. Let's go practice making sand castles. "

The two of them worked for hours, Arnold designing, building, and shaping, and Summer carrying buckets of sand and water and making admiring noises. When they were finished, the result was magnificent.

"Arnold, it's so beautiful. All it needs is a little something on top. . . ." Summer looked around. Then she picked up something. "Ooh, Arnold, look at this." She showed him a pink heart-shaped shell. Summer carefully placed it on top of the highest turret of the sand castle.

"Wow. It's great," Arnold said. He looked

into Summer's eyes. "Summer, do you think we'll see each other after this week?"

"Oh, Arnold, what we have is so strong and so deep that nothing can ever take it away from us." She kissed him on the cheek.

Just then Sandy strolled up to them. "Whoa . . . killer work, dudes."

"Thanks," Summer said. "We're thinking of signing up for tomorrow's sand castle competition. Right, Arnold?" she smiled at him.

"Uh, I don't know . . . ," Arnold said.

Summer raised her eyebrows at Sandy, silently urging him to speak. He looked at her, then back at Arnold. "Come on, you're really good, man."

Summer batted her eyelashes at Arnold. "So what do you say, Arnold?"

Arnold smiled at her. "Let's do it!"

CHAPTER 9

The next day Arnold arrived early at the sand castle competition. He waited under the banner for Summer.

In the dunes behind him, Helga miserably watched Arnold. Suddenly she heard the sound of a moped and turned to see Sandy and Summer riding up on it. They stopped behind a dune, out of sight from Arnold.

Helga raced down to Arnold and yanked on his arm. "Arnold . . ."

"Forget it, Helga. Go away. I'm waiting for Summer."

"But, Arnold . . . she's over there." Helga pointed toward the dunes. Arnold looked curiously at Helga, then let her pull him by the arm. When they got near the place where Summer and Sandy had parked, Helga drew Arnold down behind a bunch of grass.

Sandy climbed off his moped. "So you're sure he doesn't have a clue?" he asked Summer.

"Arnold? No way." Summer laughed. "He's pathetic. He's in love with me. I could probably get him to build me five sand castles."

"But we just need one, baby," Sandy said, confused.

"I know. One sand castle, we get first prize, I totally blow off Arnold, and I get to be on *Babewatch*!" Summer giggled. "This plan has worked so perfectly!" She leaned over to kiss Sandy.

Helga watched Arnold sadly. He looked stricken, like his world had just fallen apart. "Sorry, Arnold," she whispered.

Arnold was silent for a long while. "You were right the whole time, Helga," he finally said in a quiet voice.

Summer walked toward them, alone. "Oh, Arnold," she said, surprised, "there you are." She smiled brightly. "Ready to build our winning sand castle? I could hardly sleep last night thinking of you, well, actually, us!"

Arnold stood up. "Forget it, Summer. I'm on to you. I know you think I'm pathetic and an idiot, and I know you've been lying to me this whole time."

Summer blinked, stunned at being found out. "Arnold, I don't know what you're talking about—"

"You know exactly what I'm talking about. I just heard you and that guy. You were using me this whole time."

"But-But . . . ," stammered Summer.

"So I'm not building any sand castle with you, ever. Good-bye, Summer." Summer stood in shock, her plan crumbled to nothing.

"Bye, Autumn," Helga said, smiling. "It's been a blast! Too bad your evil scheme fell flat on its face." Then she ran to catch up with Arnold.

Arnold glanced at Helga. "Sorry I didn't listen to you, Helga. I thought you were making it all up. But I guess you were really trying to"—he stopped, surprised by the thought—"be my friend."

Helga blinked and waved her arms bashfully. "Yeah, well, I figured it was the right thing to do; I mean, she was taking advantage of you, and I couldn't just let her—"

Helga suddenly stopped herself from confessing her true feelings to the boy she loved. She was being way too honest. Instead she pretended to be all business.

"Hey, what are we doin' standing around here for? We're wasting time! We've got a sand castle competition to win!"

Arnold brightened up. "Yeah, let's go."

CHAPTER 10

When the sand castle contest got underway, Arnold and Helga worked perfectly together. They built a magnificently ornate walled city of towers and turrets. Its crowning feature was a strong, stately sand bridge between the two tallest towers.

Meanwhile, Sandy and Summer worked on their sand castle nearby, but spent more time throwing wet sand at one another. By the end of the contest they had nothing but a series of small hills and pits to show for their work. Summer was in tears and Sandy was furious.

"The winners of this year's sand castle competition are Arnold and Helga!" called the contest judge. The crowd cheered, cameras flashed, and Arnold and Helga stood together, beaming.

"For first prize, both of you will appear on the hit TV show *Babewatch,* filmed right here on our beach!"

Helga stepped forward and shot a gloating look at Summer. "That's right," Helga yelled. "Me! I'm the winning girl!"

Summer wailed loudly. Sandy attempted to comfort her, but Summer elbowed him hard in the stomach.

That evening as the sun set, Helga stood just off camera on the *Babewatch* beach location, ready for her big entrance.

"And . . . action!" yelled the director.

First the hunky male lifeguard ran onto the beach, followed by the strapping blond female lifeguard and then by Helga, who was also wearing the regulation *Babewatch* orange swimsuit, even though hers was a couple of sizes too big.

The three of them stared intently at the sea, where a typical *Babewatch* victim was fighting for his life in the surf. It was Arnold, who was doing an impressive job of flailing.

The first lifeguard swam athletically out to Arnold and hauled him to shore. Then the woman lifeguard moved into position to pretend to resuscitate him. Suddenly Helga leaned in and pushed her out of the way.

"Move over, Barbie, I've got this one," Helga said. She knelt down next to Arnold and puckered up, ready to deliver the breath of life.

As she bent to put her lips to Arnold's, Helga knew this moment was definitely the highlight of her vacation. Actually, when she thought about it, it was the highlight of her life.

about the authors

Hey Arnold! creator Craig Bartlett was born in Seattle, Washington. He wanted to grow up to be either an artist or a secret agent, but became an animator instead. He moved to Los Angeles in 1987 to direct the Penny cartoons for *PeeWee's Playhouse*. Craig stayed to write and direct on the first season of *Rugrats*, which introduced him to his friends at Nickelodeon. He premiered his first episode of *Hey Arnold!* on Nick in 1996, and has since made 100 episodes. He lives with his wife, Lisa, and kids, Matt and Katie, in Glendale, California, and enjoys painting, snorkeling, and reading the *New Yorker* magazine, preferably in Hawaii.

Maggie Groening was born in Portland, Oregon, where she grew up wanting to be a writer and watching a lot of TV. She moved to New York City in 1983, and worked as a writer for the Children's Television Workshop, Disney, and many textbook companies. In 1991 she wrote the Maggie Simpson book series with her brother and co-author Matt Groening. She lives in Brooklyn, New York, with her husband, Potter; her children, Franklin and Louise; and a crabby cat.